The **Bear** Collection

This book belongs to

....

SIMON AND SCHUSTER
First published in Great Britain in 2014 by Simon and Schuster UK Ltd
1st Floor, 222 Gray's Inn Road, London, WC1X 8HB
A CBS Company

Bear Wants More previously published in 2003, *Bear Feels Ill* previously published in 2007
and *Bear Says Thanks* previously published in 2012, all as individual titles.

Text Copyright © 2003, 2007 and 2012 Karma Wilson
Illustrations Copyright © 2003, 2007 and 2012 Jane Chapman

A CIP catalogue record for this book is available from the British Library upon request

ISBN: 978-1-4711-2240-8

Printed in China

2 4 6 8 10 9 7 5 3 1

www.simonandschuster.co.uk

The **Bear** Collection

karma wilson & jane chapman

SIMON AND SCHUSTER

London   New York   Sydney   Toronto   New Delhi

The **Bear** Collection

karma wilson & jane chapman

Bear Wants More

Bear Feels Ill

Bear Says Thanks

To my husband and best friend, Scott,
who loves my cooking so much, he always wants more
– KW

For Tim and Noah, with love
– JC

Bear Wants More

When springtime comes,
in his warm winter den
a bear wakes up
very hungry and thin!

He waddles outside
and roots all around.
He digs and he paws
fresh shoots from the ground.

He nibbles on his lawn
till the last blade is gone.
But
the bear
wants more!

Mouse scampers by
with his acorn pail.
"Come along," Mouse squeaks,
"to Strawberry Vale!"

So up Mouse hops
onto Bear's big back.
They tromp through the woods
for a fresh fruit snack.

The berries grow sweet, and they eat, eat, EAT!

But
the bear
wants more!

The noon sun glows,
when along hops Hare.
"Good day, friend Mouse!
How do, friend Bear?"

"I'm HUNGRY!" roars Bear.
Hare says, "Follow me!
There's a fresh clover patch
by the cottonwood tree."

They nibble on their lunch,
with a crunch, crunch, **crunch!**

But
the bear
wants more!

Badger shuffles by
with his new fishin' pole.
"There's a fine fish feast
at the ol' fishin' hole."

They head to the pond
and they sit by the shore.
Bear catches fish,

. . . but
he still
wants
more!

Meanwhile ...
back at the big bear's den
wait Gopher and Mole
with Raven and Wren.

They bake honey cakes.
They decorate the lair.
It's a springtime party
for their good friend Bear!

Bear rubs at his tummy.
He smells something YUMMY ...

and he still
wants
more!

Bear sniffs and he snuffles
as a sweet breeze blows.
He romps to his home.
He follows his nose.

His friends yell "SURPRISE!"
when he gets to his den.
But Bear is SO big . . .

. . . that he can't fit in!

Bear wails, "What luck! I am
STUCK, STUCK, STUCK . . .

in my own
front
door!"

Mouse squeaks, "Poor Bear.
He is wedged too tight."
Hare tugs, Raven pushes
with all of their might.

Badger gets a stick
and he pries SO hard . . .

... that Bear POPS out
and he lands in his yard!

Since Bear is SO WIDE, they party outside.

And he still wants more!

Bear opens presents;
he gobbles honey cakes.
He eats SO much
that his big tummy aches.

He snuggles in the grass
And he snores big snores.
He is full, full, full . . .

but . . .
his friends
want more!

Bear Feels Ill

To Debi, Mark, Addie and Stephanie:
Dearest family, I hope you always
feel your best. God bless!
– KW

To Noah and Levi,
who once made me feel sick,
but now only ever make me feel better.
– JC

Alone in his cave
as the autumn wind blows,
Bear feels achy
with a stuffed-up nose.

He tosses and he turns,
all huddled in a heap.
Bear feels tired,
but he just can't sleep.

He sniffs and he sneezes.
He whiffs and he wheezes.
And the bear
          feels
                ill.

His friends gather round.
"Come out, Bear, and play."
Bear shakes his head.
"I'm too poorly today."

Mouse mutters, "Oh my,
Bear's head is too hot."
Hare says, "We will help!
Here's a warm, cosy spot."

Bear mumbles and he moans. He grumbles and he groans.

And the bear
feels
ill.

Mouse squeezes Bear tight.
He whispers in his ear,
"It'll be just fine.
Your friends are all here."

Badger fetches water.
Gopher cooks the broth
while Mole soothes Bear
with a cool, wet cloth.

They cover Bear up and he drinks from a cup.

But he still feels ill.

Raven says, "*Caw!*
Come along, Owl and Wren.
Let us go gather herbs
to bring back to the den."

They coax Bear to sip
just a smidgen of tea.
"You'll feel better soon,"
says Mouse. "Wait and see."

Bear shakes and he shivers. He coughs and he quivers.

And he still feels ill.

The friends fuss and fret.
The friends cook and care.
They keep a close eye
on their poor ill Bear.

They all talk in whispers.
They walk on tippy toes.
They sing lullabies.
Then the bear starts to doze.

They watch Bear for hours.
"We've done all we could."

Then the bear wakes up.

And the bear
feels
GOOD!

Bear cries, "I'm all better.
I'm feeling like new.
I'm not hot and achy.
It's all thanks to you!

"Let's celebrate now.
Let's go out and play.
Let's jump in the leaves.
Let's frolic all day!"

Then Mouse starts to wheeze and Hare starts to sneeze . . .

and the friends
feel
ill!

Bear murmurs, "Don't worry,"
and tucks them in bed.
He bundles them up
and he kisses each head.

He tells all his friends,
"You'll soon feel like new.
You took care of me . . .
now I'll take care of you."

Bear Says Thanks

All alone in his cave,
Bear listens to the wind.
He is bored,
bored,
bored . . .
and he misses his friends.

"I could make a big dinner!
A feast I could share."

But he looks through his cupboard,
and the cupboard is bare.

Then Mouse stops by with a huckleberry pie.

And the **bear** says, "Thanks!"

Bear says, "Goodness me,
a delectable pie!"

"But I have made nothing,"
he adds with a sigh.

Then they hear, "Hi ho!"
and they both see Hare
with a big batch of muffins
at the door of the lair!

Hare hurries in from the cold, rushing wind . . .

and the bear says, "Thanks!"

"Of course!" says Hare.
Then he points to the door.

"Here comes Badger.
He's got even more!"

"Brrrrr!" says Badger
as he tromps inside.
He sets down his pole
and he smiles real wide.

"I'm back from a stroll at the old fishin' hole!"

And the bear

says,

"Thanks!"

Then Gopher and Mole
tunnel up from the ground.
"We have warm honey nuts.
Let's pass them around!"

There's a flap and a flitter
and a flurry in the den
when in flutters Owl
with Raven and Wren.

"We have pears from the tree
and herbs to brew tea!"

And the bear
says,
"Wait . . ."

Bear mutters and he stutters
and he wears a big frown.
Bear sighs and he moans
and he plops himself down.

"You have brought yummy treats!
You are so nice to share.
But me, I have nothing.
My cupboards are bare!"

Mouse squeaks, "Don't fret.
There's enough, dear Bear.
You don't need any food,
you have stories to share!"

His friends hug him tight. "It will be all right!"

And the bear

says,

"Thanks!"

They lay out their feast
on a quilt on the ground.
And the bear takes a seat
while his friends gather round.

In a cave in the woods,
in a warm, bright lair,
the friends feel grateful
for their good friend Bear.

They pass around platters.
They tweet and they chatter . . .

and they **all** say, "Thanks!"

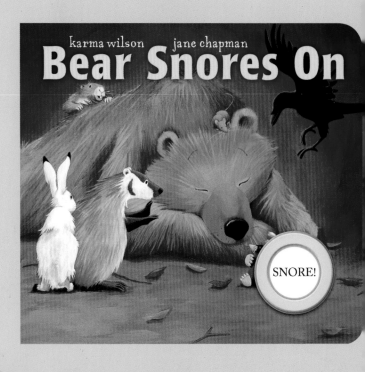

karma wilson   jane chapman

Bear Snores On

SNORE!

Discover more about Bear and all his friends.

Bear Feels Scared

karma wilson   jane chapman

The creators of the internationally bestselling Bear Snores On

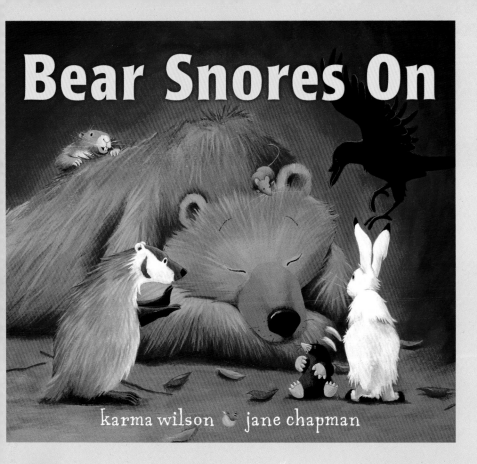

Bear Snores On

karma wilson · jane chapman

karma wilson   jane chapman

Bear's New Friend

Join Bear and his friends for the holidays!

karma wilson · jane chapman

Bear Stays Up

FOR CHRISTMAS

From the creators of the bestselling
Bear Snores On

karma wilson · jane chapman

Bear's Loose Tooth